O'BRIEN panda cubs

PANDA CUBS SERIES
where rea

D1514088

O'BRIEN SERIES FOR YOUNG READERS

Hal's Sleepover

Words: Maddie Stewart
Pictures: Greg Massardier

THE O'BRIEN PRESS
DUBLIN

First published 2008 by The O'Brien Press Ltd,
12 Terenure Road East, Dublin 6, Ireland
Tel: +353 1 4923333; Fax: +353 1 4922777
E-mail: books@obrien.ie
Website: www.obrien.ie

ISBN 978-1-84717-034-7

British Library Cataloguing-in-Publication Data
A catalogue reference for this title is available
from the British Library

1 2 3 4 5 6 7 8 9 10
08 09 10 11 12 13 14 15

The O'Brien Press receives
assistance from

Typesetting, layout, editing: The O'Brien Press Ltd
Printed by Livonia Print, Latvia

Can YOU spot the

panda cub

hidden in the story?

THUD. THUD. THUD.

'Mammy, Mammy,' said Hal.
'There's a **dinosaur**
in the hall!'

'Don't be silly, Hal,'
said Danny.
'It's me.
I'm bumping
my **sleepover bag**
down the stairs.'

'I'm going to a
sleepover party!'

Hal jumped up
to see.
'That's a huge bag!
What's inside?'

Danny had a list.

torch
false face
chocolate milkshake
buns
biscuits
party cake
sleeping bag
wash bag
pyjamas

12

'Wow!' said Hal.
'What do you do
at sleepover parties?'

'You stay up **real late**,'
said Danny.
'You watch a great **movie**.
You play **party games**
in the dark.'

'I like **Torchlight Chasies** and **Burglar Bill**.'

'You make
shadow pictures
and throw **sponge balls**,'
said Danny.

'You eat **chocolate cake** and all sorts of **buns** and **sweets**.'

'Then, when it's
very, very late,'
said Danny,
'you snuggle down
in your **sleeping bag**
and laugh and talk
until you fall asleep.'

19

Hal was excited.

He clapped his hands.

'I'm going with you,' he said.

'Don't be silly,' said Danny.
'You can't come.
You're too small.'

'I am NOT too small!
I want to go
to the sleepover party,'
said Hal.

'Mammy, please, please, please, can I go
to the sleepover party?'

'No, Hal, you can't.
You're too young.
Anyway, you're not invited,'
said Mammy.

Big wet tears
dripped down Hal's cheeks.
'But I really, really, really
want to go.'

'Well, you can't,' said Danny.

TAP. TAP.

'Granny's here,'
said Mammy.

Hal hid his head.
He didn't want Granny
to see him crying.

'Whatever is the matter,
Hal?' asked Granny.

She sat down
and lifted him up
on her lap.

Hal put his arm
around Granny's neck.

'I want to go
to a sleepover party,'
said Hal.
'But everyone says
I'm too small.
It's not fair.'

31

'Well,' said Granny,
'I have never been
to a sleepover party,
not once in my whole life.
I suppose I am
too old now.'

'Of course not, Granny.
You can never be
too **old** for anything.'

Then Hal had a brilliant idea.
'Granny,' he said,
'why don't **we** have
a sleepover party
of our own?'

'We could have it
at my house,' said Granny.

'What a good idea,'
said Mammy.

Granny went home
to get things ready
for her first ever
sleepover party.

Hal made a list:

torch

false face

chocolate milkshake

buns

biscuits

party cake

sleeping bag

wash bag

pyjamas

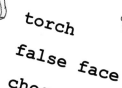

He packed
his sleepover bag.

37

Granny came back
in her little blue car.
Hal rushed out.

'Bye, bye, Mammy.
Bye, bye, Daddy.
Bye, bye, Danny.'

Hal and Granny
were off to
their very own
sleepover party.

Granny's living room
was full of party things.

Hal was delighted.
'This is **BRILLIANT**!'
he said.

41

Hal and Granny
watched cartoons.

They played
Torchlight Chasies
and Burglar Bill.

They made shadow pictures.

They threw sponge balls.

They ate chocolate cake
and all sorts of
buns and sweets.

When it was very, very late,
they snuggled down
in their sleeping bags.

'This is the best sleepover party **ever**,' said Hal.

'Ever, ever,' said Granny.

And they both
fell fast asleep.